Intergalactic Wars

Intergalactic Wars

Taking Down Sir Phantom

Josh Zimmer

Superstar Speedsters

Dedicated to Star Wars for inspiring the universe of Intergalactic Wars

The universe of Intergalactic Wars was inspired by Star Wars!

1. Justin
2. Ben
3. Flame Order Troopers
4. Supreme Leader Stardust
5. Sir Phantom

CONTENTS

book

In a galaxy far far away, Ben and his troopers patrolled the space station! Justin laid in his cell, with his arms chained to the wall. Justin used his leg, and whacked the chain cutter closer to him. Justin lifted the chain cutter in to the air, with his leg, and kicked it in to the air. Justin caught the chain cutter in his mouth, and used it to cut the chains, that were on his arms. The chains were cut, and Justin got his arms unchained. Justin got up , and walked to the door panel. Justin stabbed his vibroblade in to the door panel. The door opened, and Justin walked out of it. The Flame Order Troopers were patrolling the area. Justin sneaked through the hallway, and avoided the troopers. Justin noticed the security camera on the walls, and took his blaster out. Justin shot the security camera with his blaster. The security cameras exploded, as Justin ran through the hallway. The troopers noticed the commotion from the hallway, and spotted Justin. The troopers took out their blasters, and shot them at Justin. Justin dodged the blaster bolts, and shot the troopers with his blaster. The troopers laid on the ground in puddles of blood. Justin walked to the security room. Justin noticed that the door panel was red, and the door was locked with a security key. Justin shot the door panel with his blaster. The door panel exploded, and the door opened. Justin walked in to the security room. The security room had a bookshelf, that was filled with books, and a computer that controlled every security camera on the space station. Justin walked to the computer, and logged in to it. Justin tapped on the computer, and made every security camera malfunction in the hallway. The security cameras in the hallway malfunctioned, and exploded. The explosion killed every Flame Order Trooper on the space station. Ben saw every Flame Order Trooper laying on the ground, and growled. Ben smashed his control panel with his vibroblade. Justin watched Ben's rage on the computer. Justin logged out of the computer, and walked out of the security room. Justin walked through the hallway. Ben walked off the space station's bridge, and looked for Justin. Ben patrolled the area, and tore the security cameras off of the wall, with his powers. Justin ran through the hallway, and took out his blaster. The blaster bolts bounced off of the wall. Ben saw the blaster bolts, and deflected them with his vibroblade. The blaster bolts deflected back to Justin. Justin backflipped out of the way, and landed on the ground. Ben saw Justin and walked toward him. Ben used his powers to pull Justin toward him. Justin was struggling in Ben's grip. Ben said, "You are like a slippery little mouse, that wants to ruin the Flame order's plans for the galaxy." Justin struggled as he said, "I am slippery, and it is fun to make you rage." Ben growled, as he threw Justin in to the wall. Justin got up from the ground! Ben took out his vibroblade, and ran toward Justin. Justin backflipped, and kicked Ben in the face. Ben slid backwards, and growled. Justin landed on the ground, and took out his vibroblade. Justin swung his vibroblade at Ben. Ben dodged, and clashed his vibroblade with Justin's vibroblade. Ben backflipped, and kicked Justin in the chest. Justin slid backwards in to the wall. Ben sped in to Justin, and smashed him in to the wall. Ben swung his vibroblade through Justin's hair, and cut several pieces off of his head. Justin's hair landed on the ground, as Justin growled. Justin grabbed his blaster from his belt, and shot Ben in the chest. Ben slid backwards, as blood dripped on the ground. Ben stabbed a healing pack in to his arm. Justin sped in to Ben, and tackled him in to the ground. Justin punched Ben in the face, multiple times. Ben growled, and used his powers to electrocute Justin. Justin got electrocuted, and smashed in to the wall. Ben got up from the ground, and walked toward Justin. Justin laid next to the wall, and rubbed his head. Justin grabbed his blaster from his belt, and shot it at Ben. Ben deflected the blaster bolts from his vibroblade. The blaster bolts were deflected in to the wall. Ben sped in to Justin, and kicked him in the chest. Justin growled, and swung his vibroblade at Ben's face. The vibroblade scratched Ben's face! Ben growled, and electrocuted Justin. Justin screamed in pain, as he laid on the ground. Ben continued electrocuting Justin. Justin tried to deflect the electric energy with his vibroblade to prevent the pain from his body. Ben ignited an electric blast from his body, that covered the area with electric energy. Justin smashed through the wall, and laid on the ground, with his body being paralyzed. Justin couldn't move off of the ground. Ben laughed, as he walked toward his prey. Ben stepped on Justin's chest! Ben said, "Don't bother fighting back, you are outmatched by the strength and power of The Flame Order!" Ben grabbed Justin's neck, and picked him up! Ben smashed Justin against the wall! Justin growled, as the pain flowed through his body. Ben walked toward the command panel, and strapped Justin to one of the chairs with his powers. Ben said, "Watch the power of The Flame order in motion!" The rebel space fighter ships went out of hyperspace, and flew toward the space station. The Flame Order space fighter ships surrounded the rebel space fighter ships. The Flame order space fighter ships shot their weapons at the rebel space fighter ships. The rebel space fighter ships exploded! The rebel space fighter ships sent reinforcements. The rebel commander ship went out of hyperspace, and started firing at The Flame Order space fighter ships. The Flame Order space fighter ships exploded, and the rebel commander ship started firing at the space station. Ben pressed some buttons on the control panel, and the space station's laser charged up. Ben pressed the button on the control panel, and the space station laser fired at the rebel commander ship. The rebel commander ship exploded, as Ben smiled at the destruction. Justin was terrified in fear! Ben said, "This is why, you don't mess with The Flame Order!" The Flame Order flight ship flew out of hyperspace, and landed on the space station. Ben said, "The supreme leader is here to congratulate me on my performance." Supreme Leader Stardust walked on to the bridge of the space station.

Supreme Leader Stardust walked toward Ben. Ben bowed to Supreme Leader Stardust! Justin grabbed his blaster from his belt, and aimed it at Supreme Leader Stardust. Justin shot Supreme Leader Stardust with his blaster. Supreme Leader Stardust growled and said, "You tried to kill me!" Supreme Leader Stardust electrocuted Justin and Ben with his electric powers. Justin got electrocuted, and Ben deflected the electricity with his vibroblade. Supreme Leader Stardust deflected the electricity with his vibroblade. Ben and Supreme Leader Stardust growled at each other, as they shot their electric powers at each other. Ben threw a electric ball at Supreme Leader Stardust. The electric ball hit Supreme Leader Stardust in the chest. Supreme Leader Stardust slid backwards, and shot another strand of electricity at Ben. Ben deflected the electricity in to the wall strap. The electric powers broke the strap, that was holding Justin to the wall. Justin landed on the ground, and walked behind Supreme Leader Stardust. Supreme Leader Stardust was distracted by Ben, and didn't see Justin behind him. Justin took out his vibroblade, and stabbed Supreme Leader Stardust in the back. Blood poured on to the ground, as Supreme Leader Stardust screamed in pain. Justin took his vibroblade out of Supreme Leader Stardust's back. Supreme Leader Stardust laid on the ground in a puddle of blood. Supreme Leader Stardust's troopers walked in to the room, and pointed their weapons at Justin and Ben. The troopers started firing at Justin and Ben. Ben and Justin deflected the blaster bolts at the troopers. More troopers marched in to the room, and fired their weapons! Justin backflipped behind a trooper, and stabbed his vibroblade in to the trooper's head. Justin pulled the vibroblade out, and the trooper laid on the ground, as blood poured out of his head. Justin wiped the blood off of his vibroblade with a towel, while Ben electrocuted the troopers with his powers. Reinforcements marched in to the room! Ben created a electric ball with his powers, and threw it at the reinforcements! The reinforcement troopers exploded in the blast of electricity. The reinforcement leader, Sir Phantom, walked in to the room, and shot a electric blast at Ben. Ben backflipped over the blast, and stabbed his vibroblade in to Sir Phantom's arm. Sir Phantom smiled, as he lifted Ben in to the air with his other arm. Sir Phantom threw Ben in to the wall. Ben laid against the wall, as Sir Phantom took Ben's vibroblade out of his arm, and threw it on the ground. Justin growled, and sped toward Sir Phantom. Sir Phantom grabbed Justin's arm, and kicked him in the chest. Justin stood in place, and took out his blaster. Justin shot Sir Phantom in the chest. Sir Phantom slid backwards! Justin ran toward Sir Phantom, and stabbed him in the chest with his vibroblade. Blood dripped on the ground. Justin pulled his vibroblade out of Sir Phantom's chest. Ben used his powers to pull his vibroblade in to his hand. Ben got up from the ground. Ben sped toward Sir Phantom, and backflipped over Justin. Ben jumped in to the air, and stabbed Sir Phantom in the head with his vibroblade. Ben pulled his vibroblade out of Sir Phantom's head. Blood poured on the ground. Sir Phantom laughed, as he punched Ben in the chest. Ben smashed in to the wall. Sir Phantom said, "You think that you can defeat me, I am the most powerful trooper in the galaxy." Sir Phantom threw a electric ball at Justin and Ben. Justin blocked the electric ball with his vibroblade, as he slid backwards. The electric ball hit Ben in the chest. Ben smashed through the wall, and laid against it. Blood poured on the ground from Ben's face. Ben got up from the ground, while gripping the vibroblade in his hand. Sir Phantom said, " For being the commander of The Flame Order, you're not putting up much of a fight, you are just as weak as Commander Plasma." Sir Phantom shot his electric powers at Justin and Ben!" Justin and Ben deflected the electricity with their vibroblades. Ben growled and said, "I am not weak, My leadership fuels The Flame Order!!" Sir Phantom said, "Prove it! Prove to me and the rest of The Flame Order that you're not a weakling, that can be easily tossed around like a rag doll." Justin backflipped, and shot Sir Phantom in the head with his blaster. Sir Phantom slid backwards! Ben and Sir Phantom shot their electric powers at each other. Ben and Sir Phantom growled, as their electric powers surged as they expanded in power. The electricity covered the area, as Justin watched in shock. Justin used his electric powers to make the electric surge stronger. Ben and Sir Phantom slid to the wall, as their powers collided. The electric surge exploded, and electricity covered the area. Justin defended himself with the electric shield, that was on his belt. Sir Phantom and Ben laid on the ground, while gripping their vibroblades. Blood was pouring out of their bodies, as they slowly got up from the ground. Sir Phantom coughed, as he walked toward Ben. Sir Phantom shot lightning at Ben. Ben used his vibroblade to deflect the lightning back at Sir Phantom. The lightning hit Sir Phantom in the chest! Sir Phantom smashed through the wall, and laid on the ground. Blood poured out of Sir Phantom's body. Ben walked toward Sir Phantom, and stabbed him in the chest with his vibroblade. Sir Phantom's body laid on the ground, in the puddle of blood as he died. Ben laid against the wall, and sighed in a breath of relief, as he cleaned his vibroblade with a towel. Ben stabbed a health pack in to his arm, as he wiped the blood off of his body. Justin got up from the ground. Justin walked toward Ben. Ben shook Justin's hand. Ben said, "As a thank you for helping me defeat Sir Phantom, you are now a member of The Flame Order! As a combination of our strength, lets show the galaxy that The Flame Order is strong, and can take down anything in our path." Justin salutes Ben! Ben gives Justin his new Flame Order uniform! Justin puts on his Flame Order uniform, and stood next to Ben. Ben pressed the buttons on the control panel, and sent the space station in to hyperspace. The rest of The Flame Order ships went in to hyperspace, and followed the space station. The space station and The Flame Order troopers went out of hyperspace, and stopped at a planet, named Oceanvile. Oceanvile was filled with lush green grass and blue skies. The planet had various species of aliens and humans living peacefully. The Flame Order command ship opened fire on the planet. The aliens and humans were screaming in pain, as they got murdered by the Flame Order ships. Their bodies laid in puddles of blood. The smaller attack ships for The Flame Order flew down to the planet's surface, and opened fire on the planet's surface and the rest of the citizens, that lived on the planet. The blaster bolts from the ships tore everything on the planet's surface to shreds, and murdered all of the citizens, that were terrified in horror from the chaos. The bodies of the citizens laid in puddles of blood. Everything on the planet was destroyed, and burning to a crisp. The trees were lifeless, and didn't have any branches or leaves on them. The Flame Order space station activated its laser, and the planet exploded in to millions of pieces. The Flame Order ships flew back in to space, and landed on the space station. Ben and Justin smiled, as they watched the chaos outside the space station's window. The Flame Order troopers stood in place behind them, and saluted Ben and Justin. Ben said, "The galaxy has felt the wrath of The Flame Order!" Justin said, "The Flame Order will destroy everything in its path." The troopers marched in place, as Justin bowed. Ben put his vibroblade on Justin's shoulder, and knighted him as a commander. Justin stood up, as Ben lifted his vibroblade in the air. Justin held out his hand. Ben gave Justin a red crystal for his vibroblade. The red crystal laid in Justin's hand. Justin took his vibroblade off of his belt, and put the red crystal in to the compartment. The vibroblade set off a red glow, as Justin closed the compartment. Justin put the vibroblade on his belt. The troopers saluted Justin, as he took his vibroblade off of his belt, and lifted it in to the air.

Josh Zimmer is an crazy individual with an extreme imagination. He loves to have fun by listening to music, writing stories, and playing video games of various genres such as platforming, multiplayer online games, role playing games, and sports games. His favorite technology brands are Nintendo and Microsoft. They are wonderful role models for the industry. He commands an army of cats to his will with hugs, love, and snacks. He makes the cats purr and meow with happiness.